FIND ME IN
SARATOGA

Inspired by
The Early History, Mystery, and Folklore
Of Saratoga Springs, New York

Written by Patrice Mastrianni

Illustrations by David F. Globerson

Published in 2025 by
Saratoga Springs Publishing, LLC
Saratoga Springs, NY 12866
www.SaratogaSpringsPublishing.com
Printed in the United States of America

ISBN-13# 978-1-955568-61-6
ISBN-10# 1-955568-61-8
Library of Congress: On file with publisher
Text and Illustrations Copyright 2025 Patrice Mastrianni

Written by Patrice Mastrianni
Illustrations by David F. Globerson

For additional information, book sales or events contact us at
www.FindMeInSaratoga.com
E-mail: FindMeInSaratoga@gmail.com

This book is dedicated to
Miles and Henry
who love to explore the landmarks
of Saratoga Springs with the
ducks and squirrels.

Discover Saratoga and Saratoga Arts made this book possible through the Community Arts Regrant Program, funded by the New York State Council on the Arts with the support of the office of the Governor and the New York State Legislature.

Table of Contents

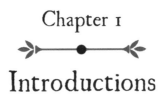

Chapter 1

Introductions

My name is Henry and I am a duck.

I live in Saratoga Springs, New York. Most of my time is spent in Congress Park, right in the middle of town.

I love to waddle around and explore the historic buildings, statues, and landmarks of Saratoga. They remind me of the brave and curious people who created this beautiful town.

Long ago, history was recorded in diaries and letters or told from person to person. Most of Saratoga's earliest historical details have been proven, but some are called "folklore."

Let's stroll around together. I'll tell you some of the facts and folklore of Saratoga's history. There's a map in the back of the book so you can find the landmarks for yourself! Each one has a "Find Me" number like this:

Find Me
#

I am Miles. I'm a squirrel.

I live in Congress Park too. Squirrels also like to explore historic landmarks. We are very curious — and sometimes a little bit mischievous. We have a different view of the history of Saratoga Springs.

I've learned that sometimes history can be a little scary, creepy, or sad, but it's always fascinating. You can count on me to have the best tails, I mean tales — because Saratoga's squirrels are totally nuts about history!

Chapter 2

Before Saratoga Springs

Long before Saratoga Springs was visited by European settlers, it was home to several Native Nations. The Mohican people settled here thousands of years ago, followed by the Mohawk and the Abenaki. They found clean, cool water seeping from the ground from what we now call springs. Spring water kept them healthy.

One spring was located below a high rocky ledge at the north end of what would become Saratoga Springs. Minerals in the water created a stone cone around the spring. Deer liked to lick salt that formed on the cone making this a good hunting spot. The Natives regarded this spring as sacred. It was known as the Medicine Spring of the Great Spirit. Colonial explorers would call it High Rock Spring.

The Mineral Cone of High Rock Spring

3

The origin of the name "Saratoga" is believed to have come from Native words such as "Soragh-aga" meaning "salt springs" or "Saragh-aga" meaning "swift water." This was probably because there is a lot of water here!

Deep below Saratoga, there is a big crack called a "fault line" in the Earth's crust. It pushes spring water to the surface through a variety of minerals. Some water smells like rotten eggs. Some springs contain carbonic gas, making the water bubbly like soda.

Long ago, people didn't know that minerals play an important role in our health. Each of the springs in Saratoga provides a different type of mineral water with its own health benefits.

Some spring water contains the mineral magnesium which relieves constipation. It actually helps people poop!

Chapter 3

How the Europeans Arrived

During the 1600s, European settlers arrived at American ports like New York City and Boston. Waterways such as the Hudson River allowed settlers to travel inland towards Saratoga, but it was still a long trip.

While coastal towns grew quickly, Europeans would not settle in Saratoga Springs for another hundred years.

Canada

Saratoga Springs

Hudson River

Boston

New York City

Atlantic Ocean

In the mid-1700s, France and Britain fought over the lakes and rivers between Canada and the Colonies. These battles slowed exploration around Saratoga. Finally, Britain took control of the waterways, allowing colonists to travel inland.

Native people from both Canada and America fought in these early battles. Many lost their lives and thousands more caught European diseases. The number of Natives decreased and sadly, Europeans took much of their land.

A colonial leader named Sir William Johnson ran a trading business west of Saratoga, along the Mohawk River. He became very friendly with the Mohawk people who lived there. A well-respected Native woman named Molly Brant became his wife.

In 1756, Sir William was appointed British Superintendent of Indian Affairs for the Northern District. He and Molly negotiated land agreements between Native tribes and colonists. Sir William believed that the Native people should be paid fairly for their land. Unfortunately, not everyone agreed.

Sir William Johnson

It is said that his friendship with the Mohawk people led Sir William to the mineral waters of Saratoga. The story goes that in the mid-1700s Sir William became very ill. His Mohawk friends felt that water from the Medicine Spring of the Great Spirit would help. They carried Sir William on a stretcher to High Rock Spring. After a few days, he began to improve.

Find Me
1

Sir William Johnson could not wait to tell his comrades about the mineral waters of Saratoga. This news brought more visitors to the region.

In 1773, a Dutch settler named Dirck Schouten built a primitive cabin overlooking High Rock Spring. This is believed to be the first colonial dwelling in Saratoga. Dirck didn't stay long, but his cabin was left behind and

Dirck Schouten's Cabin

used by other settlers before it was taken down.

Chapter 4

The Revolutionary War

In 1760, King George III ruled Great Britain and Colonial America. He charged taxes on everything that was shipped to the colonists to build a life in America. They resented his greed.

In 1776, the 13 American colonies declared their independence from Great Britain. This started the Revolutionary War. Battles occurred throughout the colonies, including New York.

Most Colonial men had no military experience and served in the war without adequate uniforms or supplies. Fighting in the Army

for America's independence was very difficult.

The Commanders of the Colonial Army near Saratoga Springs were General Horatio Gates and Major General Benedict Arnold.

General Gates was as sneaky as a squirrel! He secretly asked Alexander Bryan, an innkeeper from Waterford, NY, to spy on the British Army.

On a cold September night in 1777, Bryan went to the British camp of General John Burgoyne. It was in Fort Edward near the Hudson River. He learned that the British were planning an attack on General Gates' camp in Saratoga! When he left to warn General Gates, he was chased by a group of British soldiers.

Alexander Bryan Hiding in the Hudson River

Alexander hid in the chilly waters of the Hudson until the coast was clear. He finally reached the camp of General Gates and shared the news. This gave the Colonial troops near Saratoga time to build up their forces and prepare for the attack.

8

The Battles of Saratoga were fought on September 19 and October 7, 1777. The Colonial troops were so strong, Burgoyne surrendered. This is known as the turning point of the American Revolution. France soon agreed to support the colonists. Many more battles would be fought, but In 1783 Britain finally granted America its independence.

Find Me # 3

Burgoyne's Surrender after the Battles of Saratoga

If you want to see the Saratoga Battlefield, you still can! It is a historical landmark in Stillwater, NY, with cannons like the ones used in the Battles of 1777.

A prominent military leader named General Phillip Schuyler had a family home in Albany and a country estate in Old Saratoga, near the battlefield. This area would become the village of Schuylerville.

Around 1783, General Schuyler visited Saratoga. He built a small cabin at High Rock and spent many summers enjoying the springs.

Find Me
2

General Schuyler built a log road from Schuylerville to Saratoga. He brought other military and political leaders to the springs. The most memorable visitor was George Washington. It is said that Washington was so impressed, he tried to buy High Rock Spring but his request was denied.

In 1789, General Schuyler was elected as New York's first Senator. His political ally was Alexander Hamilton, who would serve as the US Secretary of the Treasury. You've probably seen Hamilton's picture on our $10 bill.

Hamilton married General Schuyler's daughter, Eliza. She claimed that Saratoga was her favorite place to visit!

Alexander Hamilton

Both of General Phillip Schuyler's homes in Albany and Schuylerville are seasonally open to the public.

General Schuyler lost his seat in the Senate to Aaron Burr. General Schuyler and Alexander Hamilton were against Aaron Burr's politics.

By 1804, Aaron Burr had become Vice President under Thomas Jefferson. Hamilton spoke out against Burr. His comments were published in an Albany newspaper. Burr was furious and challenged Hamilton to meet him in New Jersey for a duel. Duels were an old-fashioned way for gentlemen to settle an argument — and the argument could end with someone being shot.

Alexander Hamilton and Aaron Burr at the Duel

In the duel, Aaron Burr killed Alexander Hamilton! This ruined Burr's career. Wait until you hear what happens to Burr in the future history of Saratoga Springs!

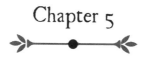

Chapter 5

Saratoga Springs is Settled

In 1787, war hero Alexander Bryan built a blacksmith shop and tavern above High Rock Spring. He is recognized as the first permanent colonial resident of Saratoga Springs. This area became known as the "Upper Village."

Over the years, the Bryan property was used as a private home and a laundry house. Two Hundred years after Bryan first arrived at High Rock, the tavern was reopened as today's popular restaurant, the Olde Bryan Inn.

Find Me # 2

The Olde Bryan Inn

Today, a steep staircase of 57 steps connects the Inn to High Rock Spring, but it's worth the trip to take a sip!

Rumor has it that the Olde Bryan Inn is haunted! Both visitors and staff claim to have seen a woman in a long, green colonial dress. She quietly appears and then vanishes without a sound. They call her Beatrice.

In 1789, Saratoga Springs had about a dozen homes. An entrepreneur named Gideon Putnam and his wife, Doanda, came to Saratoga to build a new life. An entrepreneur is someone who starts a business with confidence that it will succeed. The first business he started was making wooden shingles in the area of Saratoga now called Birch Run.

Gideon was always looking for new business opportunities. He was inspired by the nearby resort town of Ballston Springs, now called Ballston Spa. It also had mineral springs and welcomed many summer visitors seeking treatment for various illnesses. Ballston Springs featured numerous inns. In 1803, a grand hotel named Sans Souci was built there. Gideon Putnam decided to turn Saratoga into an even better health resort town.

Find Me
4

The Sans Souci Hotel of Ballston Springs in the Early 1800s

13

Gideon built Putnam Tavern and Boarding House in what was called the "Lower Village". This would give visitors a place to stay when visiting Saratoga Springs. Everyone thought his tavern would be a flop, but they were wrong!

Find Me # 6

Chapter 6

Building a Resort Town

In the 1800s, people around the country longed to take rejuvenating retreats during summer months. We now call them vacations. People learned that Saratoga Springs offered mineral water, fresh country air, and relaxation. Word spread fast that Saratoga Springs was a wonderful resort town.

To get to Saratoga in 1807, guests took a steamboat from New York City to the Port of Albany. Then they rode horse-drawn carriages on bumpy dirt roads from Albany to Schenectady, and then from Schenectady to Saratoga. The trip could take three or four days.

Find Me # 7

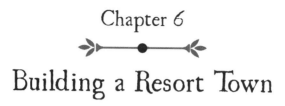

It was a long and uncomfortable journey that could only be done in warmer months. When visitors arrived, they would stay for the entire summer. Gideon's boarding house quickly filled up!

With the profits from his lumber business, Gideon Putnam purchased more land. He and Doanda laid out Saratoga as the perfect resort town.

Down the middle of the property, Gideon placed the wide Broad Street (now called Broadway) to connect the Upper and Lower Villages. Side streets led to various mineral springs.

Gideon also made space for a church, a school, and a small cemetery. He divided the land into plots that could be sold to the future residents of Saratoga.

Find Me #8

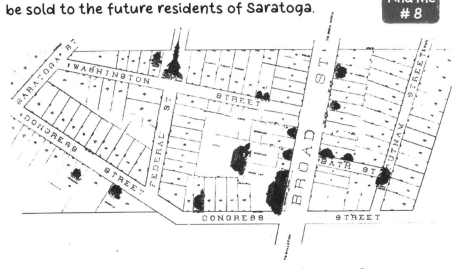

Gideon Putnam's Original Design for Saratoga Springs

The City of Saratoga Springs has grown a lot over the years. But if you look closely, you'll see that Gideon's original map is still at the heart of this special town.

Gideon added bedrooms and dining rooms to his Boarding House, but the town needed more places for guests to stay. In 1811, he decided to build a bigger hotel near Congress Spring. He named it Congress Hall. It was on the corner of Broadway and Bath Street, which is now called Spring Street.

Find Me # 9

While Gideon was inspecting the construction of Congress Hall, he fell off the scaffolding. He never healed from his injuries and died at the age of 49. No one imagined that Gideon would be the first person laid to rest in his cemetery called "Putnam Burying Ground".

Find Me # 10

Gideon and Doanda Putnam's Gravestone

Chapter 7

Where Saratoga Buried Its Dead

The lives of early settlers were often cut short due to illness or accidents. Small towns had no hospitals and most diseases had no cure. Many lives ended before their time.

In the 1700s, a piece of Saratoga farmland was used as a cemetery. It was located on Nelson Street (later named Nelson Avenue) near High Rock Street. It was called Sadler Cemetery after the property owner. By the mid-1800s, it had become very neglected and overgrown with grass and weeds.

Sadler Cemetery was a real mess. Grave markers were broken and coffins were poking out. A notice appeared in the Saratogian newspaper asking people to retrieve the remains of family members. Coffins that were intact were moved to another cemetery. The property is now a residential neighborhood.

Find Me
11

It was reported that a group of children found a human skull and brought it to school! That's one creepy Show and Tell.

Saratoga needed a more formal location for burying the dead. In 1844, Greenridge Cemetery was created near South Broadway. It now covers 28 acres and features mausoleums and statues created by the most skilled cemetery artists of the time. Many of the early citizens of Saratoga now reside there.

Find Me # 12

Greenridge Cemetery tours are offered throughout the year. Visitors can explore the artistry of the monuments and hear fascinating stories about the people who "live" there.

OK Henry, Greenridge Cemetery is a very special place, but let's get back to the early days of Saratoga when the cemetery's first residents were still alive and well!

A Grave Marker at Greenridge Cemetery

Chapter 8

Spring Water for Sale

In 1823 another entrepreneur named Doctor John Clarke purchased Congress Spring. The land around it was wet and swampy so he drained it and created Congress Park.

Doctor Clarke was a pharmacist. He used the title of Doctor to give his spring water credibility as a "cure-all." While the medicinal benefits of mineral water were still being explored, more visitors flocked to Saratoga to "take the waters."

Doctor Clarke built the Congress Spring Bottling House near the current site of the Saratoga Arts Council. The bottling house could fill 1,200 bottles a day! Saratoga's water was shipped around the world to give people a taste of Saratoga. Doctor Clarke chose not to sell Saratoga Spring Water in Ballston Spa to lure its visitors to the nearby Saratoga resort.

Find Me #5

Congress Spring Bottling House

Thousands of glass bottles were needed to package Dr. Clarke's spring water, and shipping bottles to Saratoga was expensive. To cut costs, Dr. Clarke persuaded a bottle company to open a factory just west of Saratoga.

His bottles were embossed with the letters C and E. This stood for Congress and Empire Springs. You can find many of these bottles on display at the National Bottle Museum in Ballston Spa.

Glass bottles are made from melted sand. For glass to be clear, the sand must be free of minerals like iron. To save money, it is said that Doctor Clarke claimed dark glass protected the water from sunlight, preserving its health benefits. It was a made-up story, but people bought it!

The Congress and Empire Water Bottle

With everyone drinking so much water, you'd think that Saratoga would have had a lot of bathrooms. In the mid-1800s, houses and hotels didn't have bathrooms. People used outhouses and portable toilet bowls called "chamber pots." Most people washed themselves with just a towel and a bowl of water.

A Chamber Pot

Because of the abundance of water in Saratoga Springs, bath houses were built around town. People traveled to Saratoga to soak in tubs filled with fresh mineral water in hopes of curing a variety of aches and pains.

Today most people bathe at home, but if you want to experience a mineral water bath you still can! Bath houses in the Saratoga Spa State Park still offer the spa experience featuring Saratoga's famous spring water.

To keep up with demand, more springs were drilled. People were not aware that natural resources could be used up. Saratoga Springs would soon learn a valuable lesson — don't waste the water!

Chapter 9

The Resort Grows

In 1824, Elias Benedict built the United States Hotel on Broadway between Division and Washington Streets. It was 4-stories tall and offered premium lodging. Sadly, it was destroyed in a terrible fire forty years later.

Brothers Thomas Jefferson Marvin and James Madison Marvin, named after presidents, built a new 6-story hotel in its place. The new United States Hotel opened in 1874. The block-long porch was the summer meeting place of the nation's wealthiest businessmen, giving it the nickname Millionaire's Row. This magnificent structure stood until 1945.

The United States Hotel in the Late 1870s

The Marvin brothers created a neighborhood behind the hotel called Marvin Square. It featured large homes in an architectural style called Greek Revival.

Find Me # 15

The fronts of Greek Revival houses have enormous columns topped with a triangle called a pediment.

The neighborhood was renamed Franklin Square, after Benjamin Franklin. You will find many of these grand homes in Franklin Square today.

A Greek Revival House in Franklin Square

The Oldest House in Saratoga Springs

Find Me # 16

Nearby, you'll find a small house at 36 Franklin Street. This simple design was built in 1815. The decorative porch was added later. It is believed to be the oldest surviving house in Saratoga Springs.

In 1893, a surgeon named Dr. Ethan Deuell opened the Carlsbad Sanitarium at 6 Franklin Square. This spa treatment hotel featured mineral water baths like those he visited in Europe. It became a popular health destination.

Find Me # 17

In the late 1800s, the Saratoga Carbonic Gas Company opened near the Lincoln Bath House on South Broadway. The factory removed bubbly gas from mineral water to make soda drinks The process wasted large amounts of water and released smoke into the skies of Saratoga.

Find Me # 18

Dr. Richard McCarty ran a hospital in Saratoga. In 1905, he took the Saratoga Carbonic Gas Company to court saying that the smoke produced by the factory was bad for people's health.

Dr. McCarty asked Dr. Deuell from the Carlsbad Sanitarium to be an expert witness at the trial. As Dr. Deuell was giving his testimony, he had a heart attack and died — in front of the entire courtroom! Dr. Deuell unintentionally made a very dramatic point!

Within a few years, State legislation regulated the use of spring water to prevent the springs from running dry. This forced the Carbonic Gas Company to close.

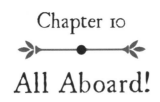

Chapter 10

All Aboard!

In 1832, a railroad connected Schenectady and Saratoga Springs. This reduced travel time for resort guests. Tracks ran through town just west of Broadway. Travelers were brought right to their hotels. It wasn't long before trains connected most American cities to Saratoga Springs.

Trains created a sharp rise in resort business. In 1820, about 1,000 summer visitors came to Saratoga. Because of trains, the resort town welcomed 13,000 guests between 1840 and 1841.

The Early Train Station of Saratoga Springs

In 1956, the Saratoga train station was moved to West Avenue. You'll find a tribute to the tracks on the sidewalks of Railroad Place. The original tracks ran up Franklin Street from what is now the Railroad Run hiking trail, to North Broadway.

Gideon Putnam's family ran his boarding house for 50 years after his death. It was expanded and renamed Union Hall. In addition to many smaller inns and boarding houses, Saratoga also featured the Congress Hotel, the United States Hotel, the Pavilion Hotel, and the Colombian Hotel.

Putnam's Union Hall was sold to the Leland Brothers, who renamed it the Grand Union Hotel. They added more rooms and a 1,600-seat opera hall. Military hero and future President General Ulysses S. Grant attended the grand opening performance on July 4, 1865.

With about 800 rooms, the Grand Union Hotel was hailed as the largest hotel in the world!

Find Me # 6

Grand Union Hotel in the Late 1800s

In the 1900s, cars made travel to Saratoga even easier, so guests began to make shorter visits. The grand hotels were no longer needed.

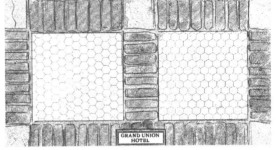

In 1952, the Grand Union Hotel was torn down and replaced by, of all things, a Grand Union market. In 1998, the market was replaced by Congress Park Centre. A section of tiles from the Grand Union Hotel floor can be found outside the apartment entrance.

Floor Tiles From the Grand Union Hotel

Find Me # 6

Chapter 11

The Cultures That Built Saratoga

Mohican Basket

Saratoga Springs was not settled by any specific ethnic or religious group, so people from different cultures were welcome. The Native residents who lived nearby sold handmade crafts in Congress Park during the early days of Saratoga.

Resort guests treasured bead work, baskets, and leather goods made by the Mohican, Mohawk, and Abenaki as souvenirs.

In the 1800s, European Immigrants came to fill Saratoga's summer jobs. Multi-family homes were built west of Franklin Square. The earliest residents were Irish, so the neighborhood was called "Dublin" after the capital of Ireland.

The Dublin Historical Marker

Italians and African Americans also worked for hotels, horse stables, and railroads. They mostly lived on Saratoga's "West Side." Small restaurants and shops made friends feel at home. Saratoga's West Side became the most diverse community in Saratoga Springs.

Even though Saratoga's East Side features very sophisticated neighborhoods, locals proudly claim that Saratoga's West Side is the best side!

The story of Saratoga's cultural history would not be complete without mentioning the food. World renowned chefs prepared gourmet meals for hotel guests, while immigrants opened neighborhood restaurants featuring international flavors.

A crispy folktale from the 1800s stars George Crum, a well-known chef of Native and African American decent. He was credited for making Saratoga's first "potato chip." The story has been disputed, but there's no doubt, Saratoga loves its potato chips! After one bite, I was hooked — nuts aren't all they're cracked up to be!

Hattie Moseley
at Hattie's Chicken Shack

The most savory story stars an African American woman named Hattie Moseley. Hattie was from Louisiana and moved to Saratoga Springs in 1938. She opened Hattie's Chicken Shack on Saratoga's West Side with just $38. She soon became the talk of the town. Hattie served both the rich and the poor, any time of day. You can still find her delicious chicken at Hattie's Restaurant, now located on Phila Street.

Find Me
21

Immigrants also opened shops along Putnam and Phila Streets. Just a few steps east of Broadway, these low-lying streets became a muddy mess when it rained. The neighborhood was later called "The Gut." There people could buy groceries, get a haircut, or have clothes mended. Sometimes rain flooded the street deep enough to row a boat!

Find Me
22

In addition to a number of shops, Jewish businessmen opened inns and bath houses on Saratoga's East Side. Saratoga Springs reminded them of the spas they visited n Europe. Jewish families frequently spent summers at the Saratoga resort.

You'll find a beautiful private home at 108 Circular Street. It was once called the Ro-Ed Mansion after the owner's children, Rose and Edward. This beautiful inn featured delicious Kosher meals, lovely gardens, and immaculate accommodations. The Ro-Ed Mansion was treasured by Saratoga's Jewish visitors.

Find Me
23

The Ro-Ed Mansion Inn

Chapter 12

Slavery Casts Its Shadow Over Saratoga

Many of Saratoga's workers came to America by choice. They were paid for working and free to come and go as they pleased. But this was not the case for everyone.

To build towns and grow food, early America needed a very large workforce. From the 1600s to the mid-1800s, European merchant ships brought thousands of poor men, women, and children, mostly from Africa, to work in America as enslaved people. They were sold to plantation owners and forced to work without pay. They were treated very poorly.

This inhumane practice was abolished in Northern States by the 1860s, but Southern States needed hundreds of thousands of people to farm their plantations. They wanted slavery to continue.

Many free African Americans worked in the hotels of Saratoga. Some even owned their own businesses. Southerners often brought enslaved workers with them when they visited. This created an uneasiness in Saratoga.

An African American named Solomon Northup was born a free man in Minerva, New York. He lived with his family in Saratoga and played violin at the United States Hotel. His wife was a well-respected cook.

In 1841, while he stood on the corner of Broadway and Congress Street, two men approached him. They asked if he'd like to play violin in New York City. He said, "Sure!" He didn't know that It was a trick!

Solomon was kidnapped and sold into slavery. He was transported to the south and made to work on a plantation in Louisiana.

Twelve years later he escaped. He told his story in a book called "Twelve Years a Slave."

In 2013, his book became an award-winning movie.

Solomon Northup

Find Me # 24

His historical marker is on Broadway at Congress St.

32

Southern plantations were so cruel and unbearable that some enslaved workers tried to escape. The Underground Railroad was a network of people who secretly guided them to freedom. It is believed that some homes around Saratoga were stops along Underground Railroad routes leading to Canada.

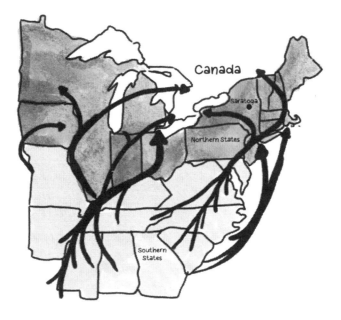

Routes of the Underground Railroad

Some African Americans were well educated and prospered in America. A New York businessman named John C. Broughton opened the Broughton House on Broadway in Saratoga Springs. It stood behind what is now St. Peter's Church. The inn welcomed upper middle-class people of color from around

the world. The Broughton House offered beautiful accommodations and performances by well-known entertainers. It was a popular destination for socialites of the day.

Find Me # 25

33

Chapter 13

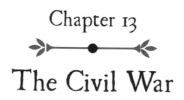

The Civil War

In 1861, The United States was made up of thirty-four states. Abraham Lincoln was President. The country was very divided on the issue of slavery. Lincoln was opposed to slavery expanding into western territories. Midwest states did not permit it. Northern states were gradually becoming emancipated and freeing enslaved people.

Southern States relied on slave labor and didn't support Lincoln's goals. They voted to secede and leave the Union to form the Confederate States of America. Two months after Lincoln took office, Southern States rebelled, which started the American Civil War.

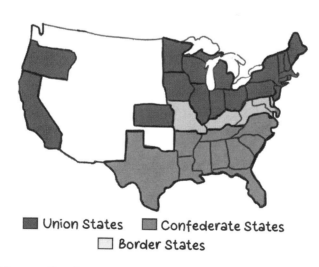

■ Union States ■ Confederate States
□ Border States

Union, Confederate, and Border States in 1861

34

Military officer Colonel Elmer E. Ellsworth was Abraham Lincoln's loyal White House assistant. He was from Malta, south of Saratoga Springs.

Soon after the country split, a Confederate flag was posted on top of a hotel near the White House. Colonel Ellsworth went to the hotel and took down the flag. After doing so, he was attacked and killed.

Colonel Ellsworth Taking Down the Confederate Flag

President Lincoln was devastated. He honored his friend with full services at the White House before his burial. Colonel Elmer E. Ellsworth is listed as the first Union soldier to be killed in the Civil War and he is honored as one of our local heroes.

35

While no Civil War battles occurred in New York State, hundreds of men from Saratoga were recruited to serve in the Union Army. The women of Saratoga sent supplies and cared for injured soldiers.

During the war, most Southerners were unable to make their annual visits to Saratoga Springs. Travel routes from the South were blocked and plantations were destroyed. This greatly reduced the number of Saratoga's summer guests.

By producing food, clothes, and weapons for Union soldiers, Northern businesses prospered.

Northerners were devastated by the country's turmoil, but they could escape it. Saratoga Springs was out of the battle zone, so wealthy Northerners continued their summer resort visits.

The Civil War was the worst war fought on American soil. It ended in 1865. Congress voted to pass the 13th Amendment to the Constitution which abolished slavery in the United States of America.

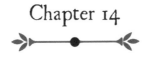

Chapter 14

Horses of the Civil War

Men didn't fight alone in the Civil War. Three million horses also served in battle. Before the war, most horses were bred for transportation. The fastest horses ran in America's oldest sport called horse racing. Sadly, many of the country's horses died in the Civil War.

In 1855, a Southern horse named Lexington was a racing celebrity. He had only lost one race. When his racing career ended, he was bred to father future champions.

Lexington

Lexington lived in Kentucky where Civil War battles were fought. To protect him from dying in the war, his owner risked his life and hid Lexington in Illinois. Luckily, Lexington survived.

The Smithsonian Institution studied Lexington's large skeleton after his death to learn what made him a champion. It remains in the International Museum of the Horse in Lexington, Kentucky. Lexington would play an important role in the future of Saratoga Springs.

During the Civil War, both Harness and Thoroughbred racing continued in New York and New Jersey, out of the battle zone. Horse owners, who could afford to, sent their best horses there to race.

If you're not familiar with horse racing, let me explain. Thoroughbred horses race with a jockey on their back. Standardbred horses run in Harness Races pulling a jockey on a cart called a sulky. The horses are different sizes and they run differently. Thoroughbred races are faster and owners can win larger amounts of money.

Harness Racing   Thoroughbred Racing

Chapter 15

Horse Racing Comes to Saratoga Springs

John Morrissey

Two years into the Civil War, a man named John Morrissey hosted four days of thoroughbred racing in Saratoga Springs.

Five thousand spectators gathered on Union Avenue around a track used for State Fair harness races. This track is now called Horse Haven.

Find Me # 26

People bet on who would win each race. Saratoga's first horse races were a big success! 1863 was a very special year in the history of Saratoga Springs.

Morrissey and a group of investors purchased 94 acres on Union Avenue for a new racetrack. They formed the Saratoga Racing Association with William Travers as the President. Saratoga Race Course opened in August 1864, and it is considered the oldest sporting venue in the country.

Find Me # 27

The first race in 1864 was called the Travers Race. It was won by a horse named Kentucky. Kentucky's father was the famous Lexington! Over the next 15 years, 9 winners of the annual Travers Race were descendants of Lexington.

Across the street from Saratoga Race Course you'll find the National Museum of Racing and Hall of Fame. The Museum exhibits artwork, photographs, and memorabilia of horse racing throughout history.

National Museum of Racing and Hall of Fame

The front of the museum is decorated with Lawn Jockey statues. These originated in the 1800s and were placed in front of homes as a greeting. The color of the Jockey's shirts, called silks, represents the stable they are racing for. Lawn Jockey statues can be found all around Saratoga Springs and in other racing towns.

You may have seen lawn jockeys in the movies! My favorite was in the Christmas movie Home Alone. A lawn jockey statue stands in front of Kevin's house. It gets hit by a car four times!

If you like impressive horse tails — I mean horse tales, here's one about a horse named Upset. The word "upset" means an unexpected result in a sports competition. No one expected that Upset was going to upset a lot of people.

In 1919, Upset was in a race at Saratoga Race Course. A famous horse named Man o' War was in the same race. Man o' War had never lost a race so everyone expected him to win.

When the race started, Man o' War was facing backwards! Upset took the lead and Man o' War couldn't catch him. Upset won and caused one of the biggest racing upsets ever seen in Saratoga.

Upset and Man o' War at the Start of the Race

Outside of the Racing Museum you'll find a statue of one of Man o' War's descendants, Seabiscuit. He was born in 1933 during the Great Depression when our country was very sad.

Find Me
28

Seabiscuit was bred to be a winner but he had stubby legs and was petrified of racing! He slept half the day and kicked the barn to bits. His owner sold him saying, "Seabiscuit is useless!"

Seabiscuit and Pumpkin

A horse trainer named Tom Smith had a feeling that this troublemaker was just misunderstood. Tom introduced Seabiscuit to a sweet pony named Pumpkin. If Pumpkin was nearby, Seabiscuit wasn't afraid.

Seabiscuit fell in love with racing, and the world fell in love with Seabiscuit. He even raced at Saratoga Race Course. His picture was on the cover of newspapers and his races were shown in movie theaters. Seabiscuit lifted the country's spirits.

Author Lauren Hillenbrand wrote a book about Seabiscuit's rise to fame. In 2003, scenes for the movie Seabiscuit, inspired by her book, were filmed in Saratoga Springs. The world fell in love with Seabiscuit all over again!

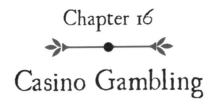

Chapter 16

Casino Gambling

After creating Saratoga Race Course, John Morrissey opened the Saratoga Club House in 1870.

Morrissey's friends loved games of chance like cards and roulette. He built his Club House in Congress Park. It is now called the Canfield Casino. The Club attracted gamblers from across the country, which brought more wealth to Saratoga Springs.

Find Me # 29

Some local residents were opposed to gambling because they felt that it could lead to crime. To build a good relationship with Saratoga, Morrissey made generous donations to local causes.

The Saratoga Club had strict rules:
No gambling on Sunday,
no women, no children,
no Saratoga residents,
and cash only!
Gambling is risky. You could win or
leave with empty pockets!

Private gambling was not legal but wealthy resort guests loved to play, so it was permitted. Today, horse racing and casino gambling are managed by the New York Gaming Commission.

John Morrissey ran the casino until he died of pneumonia in 1878 at the age of 47. He took his last breath at the Adelphi Hotel on Broadway. You can find this beautiful hotel still standing today.

Find Me # 30

The Adelphi Hotel

Some believe Morrissey's spirit never checked out. Rumor has it that one night a hotel guest was awakened by the sound of breathing on the other side of his bed. He even saw the impression of a body on the sheets! Horrified, he ran to the front desk. They explained, "Well, that is the room where John Morrissey died!"

Richard Canfield bought the Saratoga Club in 1884. He added elegant gardens and a large dining room with a stained-glass ceiling. It became known as Canfield's Casino, the most beautiful gambling hall in America.

The Stained Glass Ceiling of Canfield's Casino

Find Me # 29

In 1906, private gambling ended in Saratoga. Canfield's Casino closed, and the building sat empty. In 1911, the City of Saratoga purchased the building for $150,000 and restored it to its original beauty.

Today, the Canfield Casino hosts private events in the dining hall. On the upper floors you'll find the Saratoga Springs History Museum.

Chapter 17

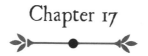

Women Who Made History

In the 1800s, only men could own property, manage money, or vote. Women had very few rights. Here are a just few stories of Saratoga women who helped change the future!

A woman named Lucy Skidmore Scribner inherited the family fortune after the death of her father and husband. In 1903, she opened a school near Congress Park called The Young Women's Industrial Club. She offered girls of all income levels the opportunity to get an education. Lucy felt that if students paid tuition,

Lucy Skidmore Scribner's Young Women's Industrial Club

they would value their education. She required that every girl pay a fee — some as little as fifty cents.

Find Me # 31

In 1922, The Young Women's Industrial Club became Skidmore College. In the 1960s, it was moved to the current 890 acre campus on North Broadway. Skidmore College is now open to both men and women. It has become one of the most prestigious colleges in New York State.

Find Me # 32

The tiny Gothic Revival House found at 166 Excelsior Avenue was

Find Me # 33

built by Sarah Smiley in 1872. She was of the Quaker faith and believed in peace and equality. After the Civil War, she traveled through the South to build schools and bring food to people of all colors. In 1875, she spoke to a large crowd at Saratoga's Grand Union Hotel. The audience included the country's Vice President and wealthy businessmen. They were all curious to meet such a wise and fearless woman.

In 1869, another trailblazer named Matilda Joslyn Gage called a meeting at Saratoga's Congress Hall Hotel to form the New York State Woman Suffrage Association. She worked to legalize a woman's right to vote. You can see her historical marker in front of Congress Park.

Find Me # 13

The Statue of Liberty

Matilda led a protest at the 1886 dedication of the Statue of Liberty. She asked this question: If women aren't allowed to vote, run a business, or own property, why is the Statue of Liberty a woman?

In the 1800s, only men went to war. But at Greenridge Cemetery you'll find one woman listed on the Spanish American War Memorial.

The Spanish American War Memorial at Greenridge Cemetery

Ruebena Walworth was from a prominent Saratoga family. She worked as a nurse in a military hospital. Diseases spread among patients and Reubena caught typhoid fever. She died in 1898 at only 31 years of age. Her mother saved a lock of her blonde hair as a keepsake.

Fifty years later, Reubena's niece, Clara Walworth, lay dying at the family home in Saratoga with an aide by her side. The aide described what happened next.

Find Me # 12

Reubena Walworth

In the glow of a candle, the aide saw the figure of a blonde woman in an old-fashioned nurse's uniform. She stood over Clara as she died, then disappeared. The aide knew that it was Reubena.

The Walworth residence was called Pine Grove and was located on Broadway near Van Dam Street. When the last family member died, the house was torn down.

Find Me # 34

The Pine Grove Historical Marker

Many of the family's furnishings, art, and personal possessions are in a permanent exhibit at the Saratoga Springs History Museum. Some visitors of the Walworth Memorial Collection believe that spirits of the family can still be felt among their possessions.

Find Me # 29

Chapter 18

>—•—<

Changes in Time

In 1868, Professor Charles Dowd and his wife Harriet opened a school in Saratoga Springs. Charles also studied time. Time was determined by the position of the sun in the sky. Trains traveled faster than sunlight. Travelers needed to adjust their watches

by minutes or hours between cities. This made train schedules confusing.

Professor Dowd proposed creating four "Standard Time" regions across the United States: the Eastern, Central, Mountain, and Pacific time zones. This system was put into use on November 18, 1883.

Charles Dowd's story also has a sad ending. Twenty-one years later, as he crossed the railroad tracks on North Broadway, he was unfortunately hit and killed by a train.

Behind the Adirondack Trust Co. on Broadway, you'll find an armillary sphere, used long ago to tell time. It pays tribute to the achievements of Professor Charles Dowd.

Find Me # 35

Charles Dowd Armillary Sphere

Chapter 19

The Architecture of Saratoga

Saratoga Springs is a showcase of beautiful buildings designed in a variety of architectural styles. In the early years of the resort town, inns and private homes were built on Saratoga's East Side. You can see architectural styles evolve from block to block.

Early building styles can be found in the oldest neighborhoods of Saratoga. If you like to count, look for houses with details like 4 columns or 3 windows. If you like shapes, look for triangles and pointed windows. Soon you'll be able to name Saratoga's Architectural styles!

Can you Find the Architectural Styles Used in the Early Days of Saratoga Springs?

Some older houses have one style, and some have two or more. Often, homeowners built additions in newer styles.

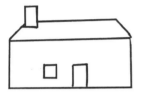

Vernacular: Made from whatever building materials are available. Design is based on climate and simple needs.

Greek Revival: The wood or stone exteriors boast a large porch. A triangle piedmont is supported by two-story columns. They are often symmetrical.

Gothic Revival: You'll find steep roofs, a front facing gable, delicate trim, and tall windows with a point on top.

Italianate: Constructed of brick or stone with three tall windows over a small porch. Corbels support the eves and cast-iron details top the roof.

Victorian: Painted in bright colors, these homes have stained glass windows, tall, pointed roofs, and a large front porch covered with fancy trim.

Second Empire: Houses are topped with a mansard roof and decorative windows. A small porch roof is supported by a couple of columns.

Queen Anne: Homes are designed with tall turrets, wrap-around porches, and large windows. Often with both brick and wood exteriors.

Craftsman: Buildings have an organic connection to the Earth with natural colors and materials. Porches often have tapered columns.

In the late-1800s, more private homes were built on North Broadway. These houses have large front lawns with a variety of architectural styles. Alleys ran behind the homes with access to carriage houses, now called garages.

Many of these houses had no heating systems. They were built just for summer use but they can now be used year-round. The North Broadway neighborhood remains a Saratoga treasure.

Find Me # 36

You might find large square stones in front of some older homes in Saratoga. They are called carriage steps. They were originally used for climbing in and out of horse-drawn carriages. No one needs them anymore, but they are too heavy to move so there they sit. Sometimes squirrels just use them for cracking nuts.

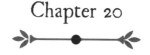

Chapter 20

Houses With Stories to Tell

If Saratoga's houses could talk, you'd hear some amazing stories!

The Queen Anne-style house found at 605 North Broadway was owned by New York State Senator Edgar T. Brackett. He was instrumental in the early growth of Saratoga. He founded a bank called the Adirondack Trust Company, which provided funding for much of what you see today.

Find Me # 37

In 1916, Senator Brackett erected a majestic building on Broadway to house his bank. It's built in a Beaux-Arts style with tall columns supporting beautiful carvings above the entrance. Tiffany & Co. created the front doors and the crystal chandeliers inside. Columns also surround the interior walls framing financial words of wisdom.

Find Me # 35

Adirondack Trust Co.

Senator Brackett worked to protect Saratoga's mineral springs by setting limits on pumping spring water. This forced the closing of the Carbonic Gas Company. It was owned by Saratoga's second mayor, Harry Pettee. Mr. Pettee wasn't happy. He built a house a few doors away from Senator Brackett's at 595 North Broadway.

Find Me
37

The Pettee house was built so the back of the house faced North Broadway. The grand front entrance faces Long Alley! Residents felt that he literally "turned his back" on Saratoga.

A few years later, Mr. Pettee told his wife he was going on a brief business trip. He left a farewell note in his safe and stole $300,000 from customers. This scandal made headlines all across the country.
He was never seen again.

Do you remember Doctor John Clarke who bottled Saratoga Spring Water? You'll find his beautiful home at 46 Circular Street overlooking Congress Park. The Greek Revival design features six huge pillars under a triangle pediment. Skidmore College purchased the Clarke mansion in 1940 to house college presidents.

The House of Dr. John Clarke

Find Me # 38

When Skidmore moved to North Broadway, they wanted to bring the Clarke house with them! They considered cutting it in half and using a helicopter to lift it over Saratoga. What a nutty idea! Today the house is still on Circular Street — and it's in one piece.

Let's find Madame Eliza Jumel's Greek Revival house at 129 Circular Street. Eliza grew up poor, but she was very clever. At 18, she met a French winemaker in Manhattan named Stephen Jumel. Supposedly, she tricked him into marriage saying that she was sick and about to die.

While he worked in France, she managed his finances in Manhattan. She made him even richer! He died at 69, supposedly from falling onto a pitchfork. She became one of the richest women in New York.

The House of Madame Eliza Jumel

After his death, Madame Jumel spent summers in Saratoga. She married the politician Aaron Burr. He's the one who killed Alexander Hamilton in the duel! Burr had become penniless. Eliza soon realized he just wanted her money. She filed for a divorce.

You'll never guess who she hired as her attorney — Alexander Hamilton, Jr.! Since Aaron Burr had killed his father in the duel, Alexander Jr. was eager to help Madame Jumel. When the divorce was final, Aaron Burr had a stroke and died!

Chapter 21

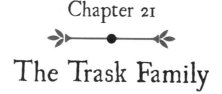

The Trask Family

Of all the people who played a major role in the history of Saratoga Springs, Spencer and Katrina Trask are the most memorable.

After graduating from Princeton University, Spencer Trask joined his uncle in financing new inventions like the telephone and the automobile. Spencer also partnered with Thomas Edison to produce the electric light bulb. His ability to recognize good ideas made him very wealthy.

In 1881, Spencer and his wife Katrina purchased a large estate on Union Avenue in Saratoga Springs. They named it Yaddo. It was filled with beautiful art and surrounded by exquisite gardens. The Trasks hosted lavish parties bringing more influential people to Saratoga Springs.

Find Me # 40

The Rose Garden Gate at Yaddo

Spencer and Katrina were extremely generous and donated to many causes. Sadly, their lives were filled with tragedy.

All four Trask children died young. And if that weren't sad enough, in 1891, the house at Yaddo was destroyed by a fire.

The Trasks didn't give up. They built a new house made of stone. Their garden features a statue named Christalan, in memory of their four children.

The Christalan Statue at Yaddo

Today, Yaddo is used as a retreat where authors, artists, and musicians can nourish their creativity. The gardens are open seasonally to the public, where visitors are surrounded with beauty and serenity.

Spencer Trask worked with Senator Brackett and the New York State Governor, Charles Evans Hughes, to pass the Anti-Pumping Act of 1908. This ruling regulated the use of Saratoga's spring water. They also established the Saratoga Reservation, now called the Saratoga Spa State Park. The park features springs, mineral baths, green spaces, and music venues. About twenty springs are still active today thanks to the efforts of these men.

Find Me # 41

On New Year's Eve 1909, Spencer boarded a train to New York City to discuss Saratoga's Springs with the Governor. While his train was at a stop, it was hit by another train. The crash resulted in Spencer's death. The world lost a brilliant visionary, and Saratoga Springs lost a treasured friend.

After Spencer's death, Katrina had a large statue made in his honor. The Spirit of Life statue was unveiled in 1915 and can be found in Congress Park.

Let's waddle back to our park and see the Spirit of Life and other historical landmarks you don't want to miss.

Hey Henry! Before you start waddling through town, we should tell everyone what happens when the ducks of Saratoga Springs are crossing the street. The rule is... everyone must STOP!

Whether there is one duck or twenty, all traffic comes to a halt. Saratoga Springs really loves their ducks. They make everyone quack up!

Chapter 22

Congress Park

Before we enter Congress Park, let's learn about the beautiful building directly across the street. Built in 1915, this was originally a trolley station. Guests arrived on electric trolleys from nearby towns and lakes. It is designed in the Beaux Arts style of architecture. Above the doors you will find the paintings of Sir William Johnson at High Rock Spring and the Battle of Saratoga.

Find Me # 42

The Trolley Station

When trolleys were no longer used, the building became a "drink hall" for tasting spring water. Today it houses the Saratoga Springs Heritage Area Visitor Center.

Now let's explore Congress Park. The entrance gate is dedicated to Senator Edgar T. Brackett in appreciation of all he did for Saratoga Springs. He loved Congress Park as much as we do. His last request was that he be driven past this gate on the way to his final resting place in Greenridge Cemetery.

Find Me
#43

Just inside the park entrance you will find the 77th Regiment Civil War Memorial. It honors Civil War soldiers from the Saratoga area. The troop requested that they be called the 77th Regiment because they were fighting to protect the Union, just like the Battles of Saratoga in 1777.

Find Me
44

The Civil War Monument

The Civil War memorial originally stood on Broadway outside the front gate. Horse-drawn carriages could easily pass around it. After an automobile accident in 1920, it was moved inside the park.

The Spirit of Life Statue

Find Me # 45

To your left, you'll find the Spirit of Life statue, in memory of Spencer Trask. It was created by artist Daniel Chester French.

The figure was inspired by Hygenia, the Greek goddess of health. She pours water from a bowl and holds up a pine branch, like those at Yaddo.

On the wall behind her are the words, "To Do Good and Serve My Fellow Man." The Spirit of Life has become the symbol of Saratoga Springs.

When Daniel Chester French finished the Spirit of Life, he created another statue in Washington, DC. Maybe you've heard of the Lincoln Memorial! That statue became the symbol of Washington, DC, as well as the United States of America.

65

If you'd like to try some mineral water, it can still be sipped from Congress Spring under the large Greek Revival pavilion near the park entrance.

Find Me # 46

The nearby Columbian Spring was discovered by Gideon Putnam in 1803.

Just past Congress Spring, look for the Deer Park Spring under a domed cast-iron fountain made in England. This spring is named after the Deer Lodge that stood nearby in the mid-1800s.

Find Me # 47

The Deer Lodge allowed visitors to see real live deer in Congress Park. A story was told that a woman didn't share her treats with one feisty deer, so he kicked her and she sued Saratoga Springs.

Eventually, the Deer Lodge closed and the deer went back to the forest.

Congress Park visitors find joy and laughter riding on the beautiful carousel created in 1910 by artist Marcus Charles Illions. He carved and painted each of the original 28 horses. He even added real horsehair tails. The carousel previously stood in nearby Kaydeross Park which closed in 1987.

Find Me # 48

A Carousel Horse in Congress Park

The carousel was abandoned and set to be auctioned off, one horse at a time. A group of Saratoga citizens joined together and saved this work of art.

In 2002, the carousel was restored and moved to Congress Park where it continues to bring smiles to riders of every age.

Richard Albert Canfield's
Initials in the Fence

Find Me
49

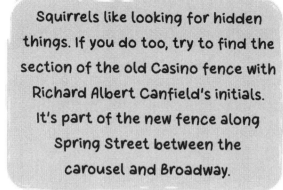

Squirrels like looking for hidden things. If you do too, try to find the section of the old Casino fence with Richard Albert Canfield's initials. It's part of the new fence along Spring Street between the carousel and Broadway.

The mineral spring called Hathorn No. 1 can be found outside the fence on Spring Street. Its strong flavor takes a little getting used to, but some sippers think it's delicious! Find Me # 50

When Mr. Canfield remodeled the Casino, he added an Italian Renaissance Garden near Spring Street. Ducks LOVE to splash in the fountain with Spit and Spat. Find these two Tritons rising out of the water spitting water at each other from conch shells!

Find Me
51

Spit and Spat Fountain

68

Just beyond the fountain is the Palladian Circle featuring replicas of mythological statues. Two of them are Satyrs (part human and part goat), and two are Maenads (female followers of Dionysus). They surround a sundial which you can still use to tell time.

Find Me
51

The Satyr Statue in the Italian Renaissance Garden

The Devil's Chair in Congress Park

Up the hill from Spit and Spat, you will find the large square stone that sits among the trees. It was intended to be the "cornerstone" for the Bethesda Episcopal Church. The church was ultimately built on Washington Street but the stone was left behind.

Find Me
52

The forgotten cornerstone became known as the "Devil's Chair" because it overlooked the Casino. It was said that the Devil could sit on it and watch the wicked antics of the gamblers below.

In front of the Casino, you can see the three-tiered Morrissey Fountain. Supposedly, when John Morrissey and his friends were gambling, you would find a ball floating on top of the fountain. It secretly said, "Come in and play." Some believe it also told Saratoga police to "look the other way."

The Morrissey Fountain

Find Me #53

Across from the Morrissey Fountain are two large cast iron vases believed to be from Denmark. They are embellished with beautiful artwork. You'll find a sleeping baby and a soaring owl. They are called Day and Night.

Find Me #53

In addition to my duck and squirrel friends, the ponds of Congress Park are home to some slippery residents. Fish love the park just as much as ducks and squirrels. But remember... No Fishing Allowed!

70

Most of my duck friends gather around the Veterans Pond near the World War Memorial. In 1882, a wooden bandstand was built for live music. In 1931, it was replaced by a stone pavilion to honor Saratoga's brave soldiers.

Find Me # 54

A nearby duck pond leads us to the Katrina Trask Welcome Gate. This staircase entrance was built in 1922 as a tribute to everything Katrina gave to Saratoga. On some of the steps you'll find pieces of stromatolite from the Petrified Sea Gardens west of Saratoga Springs. These marine algae fossils are estimated to be 490 million years old.

Katrina Trask Staircase

Find Me # 55

The Katrina Trask staircase has a lot of steps. Sometimes, energetic visitors, like squirrels, climb the 64 steps for exercise. Squirrels like to climb up and down anything and everything in hopes of finding a nut or two.

71

If you want to find more historical treasures, be sure to check out the Canfield Casino. Miles and I aren't allowed inside, but we like to peek in the windows.

The Canfield Casino hosts glamorous weddings and social events. Guests are surrounded by much of the original decor from one hundred fifty years ago.

Canfield Casino and the Saratoga Springs History Museum

Find Me # 29

Upstairs is the Saratoga Springs History Museum. Exhibits include paintings, photos, clothing, and furniture from early Saratogians. You can also see crafts made by the Mohican, Mohawk, and Abenaki.

On the third floor of the museum, you'll find the Walworth Memorial Museum and the George Bolster Collection of old Saratoga photos. The collection is mostly used by historians, but anyone can order a picture of old Saratoga for their very own.

There's a lot more in the Canfield Casino than meets the eye. People believe the building is haunted! Staff members and guests have reported mysterious happenings, like items being moved across the room and doors slamming after hours.

Door Mysteriously Held Closed
Inside the History Museum

One morning, a museum worker couldn't open the only door to an empty exhibit room. He discovered that the door was being held closed by a rolled-up rug — FROM THE INSIDE!

Some people believe after we leave this world, our spirit remains connected to things that belonged to us. The museum is filled with personal possessions from many early Saratogians. If you find ghosts scary, don't worry, these spirits seem to be very friendly. Maybe they just want us to know that they are still here.

The Canfield Casino was featured on the show Ghost Hunters (Season 6, Episode 18). It is listed as one of the most haunted buildings in the country.

EPILOGUE

So now you know much of the early history, mystery, and folklore of Saratoga Springs. We hope this leaves you curious about what happens in the next 100 years.

Even though Saratoga is constantly changing, historical groups work diligently to preserve the buildings and landmarks for future generations. It is their hope that the heart and soul of Saratoga Springs never changes.

No matter where the future takes us, Saratoga Springs will always be that special place where, thousands of years ago, mineral water just came bubbling out of the ground.

Find Me in Saratoga Landmark Map

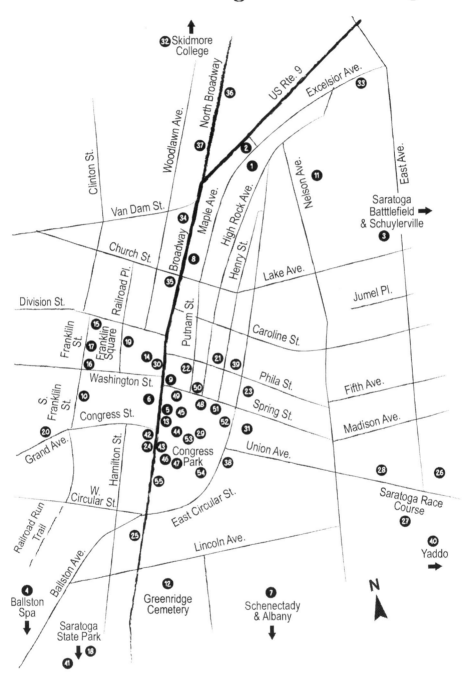

Landmark Map Directory

* Indicates where a landmark existed but is no longer there

Origin of Street Names in Saratoga Springs

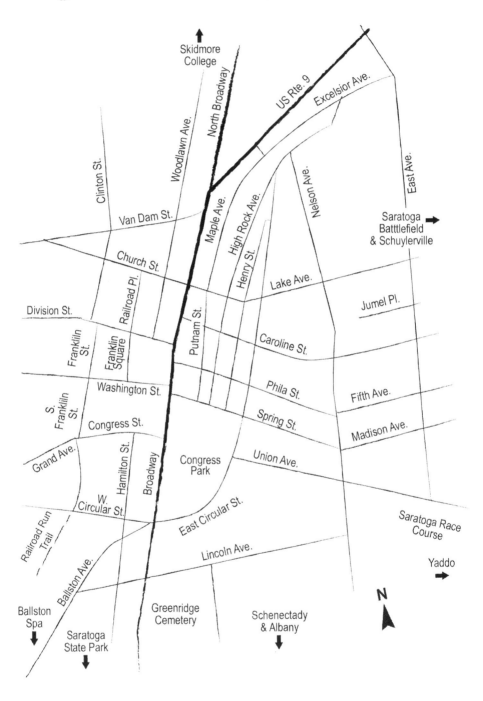

Broadway: Named by Gideon Putnam as Broad Street because it was 122 ft. wide. Wide enough to turn around a horse-drawn carriage.

Caroline St.: After either Judge Henry Walton's granddaughter or Gideon Putnam's daughter. The origin is unclear.

Church St.: Originally the location of a number of churches which were destroyed by fire or relocated. Now there are none.

Circular St.: Dr. John Clarke intended to create a street to encircle downtown, but landowners on the West Side didn't want to sell their land so it's half a circle.

Clinton St.: Named after George Clinton____ the first Governor of New York State. He served a total of 21 years in office.

Congress St.: Named after Congress Spring which was discovered in 1792 by Nicholas Gilman, a member of Congress.

Division St.: The boundary of a farm bordering the middle of Broadway.

East Ave.: Originally, the eastern border of Saratoga Springs.

Excelsior Ave.: Named after Excelsior Spring.

Fifth Ave.: Named after Fifth Avenue in New York City.

Franklin St.: Honors the politician and inventor, Benjamin Franklin.

Grand Ave.: The West Side compliment to Union Ave on the East Side.

Hamilton St.: Named after Alexander Hamilton.

Henry St.: Named after Gideon and Doanda Putnam's son.

High Rock Ave.: The location of the High Rock Spring.

Jumel Pl.: Named after Madame Eliza Jumel, a summer celebrity of Saratoga Springs.

Lake Ave.: Originally the path to Saratoga Lake.

Lincoln Ave.: Named after President Abraham Lincoln.

Maple Ave.: Originally named Front St., in 1850 it was changed to honor newly planted maple trees.

Nelson Ave.: The Nelson family farm was located out this street.

Phila St.: Named after Gideon and Doanda Putnam's daughter Phila. Not Philadelphia, as many people think.

Putnam St.: Named for Gideon Putnam.

Railroad Pl.: The original path of the railroad through town.

Spring St.: Originally called Bath St., the site of the Hamilton Bathhouse. It became Spring St. after the discovery of Hathorn Spring.

Union Ave.: Celebrates the Union after the Civil War.

Van Dam St.: The name of the Dutch recipient of land from Britain in 1708. It was part of the Kayaderosseras Patent purchased from the Native People.

Van Dorn St.: Another original Dutch owner of land in Saratoga.

Walton St.: Named after Judge Henry Walton, one of the main landowners of Saratoga Springs.

Washington St.: After Gideon's son Washington Putnam.

Woodlawn Ave.: Led to Woodlawn Park, the current site of Skidmore College.

FIND MORE STREETS IF YOU CAN!

Adams St.: Named after the 2nd President, John Adams.

Beekman St.: Named after Johannes Beekman, one of the original recipients of land that was part of the Kayaderosseras Patent.

Bryan St.: Named after Alexander Bryan, the town's first permanent European settler.

Catherine St.: Named after Phillip Schuyler's wife.

Clark St.: After Dr. John Clarke who bottled Congress Spring water and created Congress Park. The "e" was dropped.

Federal St.: Honors the birth of the United States.

Gardner Ln.: A land owner named Robert Gardner often walked this route from his property on Putnam Street to Broadway.

George St.: The brother of Caleb Mitchell, a town official.

Jefferson St.: Named after the 3rd President Thomas Jefferson.

Lafayette St.: Named after the Marquis de Lafayette, a French ally who fought in the Revolutionary War.

Lexington Rd.: Named after the famous horse, Lexington.

Madison Ave.: Named after 4th President James Madison.

Marvin Alley: Bordered property owned by the Marvin Brothers.

Monroe St.: Named after the 5th President James Monroe.

Schuyler Dr.: Named after General Phillip Schuyler.

Vanderbuilt Ave.: The wealthy Vanderbuilt family was instrumental in the growth of Saratoga.

Walworth St.: Named after the Reuben Hyde Walworth, Ruebena's father.

Whitney Pl.: This family funded many projects in Saratoga including the Race Course.

About the Author

Patrice Mastrianni has a degree in Studio Art and a passion for educating children. As an Art teacher she encourages her students to explore the world around them. Patrice is both a mom and a grandma, and takes joy in sharing her love of learning with all ages.

After owning two creative businesses in Saratoga Springs, Patrice has years of experience inspiring both residents and seasonal visitors. She also paints custom lawn jockey statues. Visit www.SaratogaJockey.com to see her artwork and portfolio. To learn more about her book or to schedule a workshop visit www.FindMeInSaratoga.com.

About the Illustrator

Dave Globerson is a graduate of the Hartford Art School and a native of upstate New York. He has spent over a decade creating custom artwork for clients, friends and family. From pet portraits to fantasy worlds, Dave's work spans watercolor, acrylic, and digital painting,

What started as small commissions during the pandemic, has grown into a full-time career, fueled by the joy that art brings to others. Whether it's a heartfelt tribute, a whimsical character, or something entirely new, Dave loves turning imagination into reality! Visit his full gallery of artwork at www.DFGIllustration.com

ACKNOWLEDGMENTS

This book was made possible with the help of many historians, story tellers and writers in Saratoga Springs. They have provided numerous resources and given hours of their time to confirm the facts and folklore presented in this book.

I wish to acknowledge the following resources:

• Saratoga Springs History Museum: James Parillo, Executive Director & Charles Kuenzel, Director of Education
• Brookside Museum: Field Horne, Acting Director and Editor in Chief of "Saratoga Springs: A Centennial History"
• City of Saratoga Springs Historian: Mary Ann Fitzgerald
• Saratoga Publishing: Chris Bushee, Editor
• Simply Saratoga Magazine: Carol Godette, author of "On This Spot"
• Saratoga Preservation Foundation: Sydney Hedge, Preservation and Programs Coordinator, and presenters of the Preservation's Sunday Strolls, namely Gloria May and Linda Harvey
• National Museum of Racing and Hall of Fame: Brien Bouyea
• Ndakinna Educational Center: Joseph Bruchac, Executive Director
• Olde Bryan Inn: John Kosek, Historian
• Greenridge Cemetery: Caroline Waldron
• City of Saratoga Department of Public Works
• Johnson Hall State Historic Site: Ian Mumpton, Interpretive Programs Assistant
• National Bottle Museum: Chris Leonard, Executive Director
• NY Parks: Jessica Serfillipi ,Schuyler Mansion
• Saratoga Springs Public Library: Saratoga Room Resource Staff, namely Donna Bates
• Skidmore College
• The Children's Museum of Saratoga
• Joe Haedrich: author of "Haunted Saratoga"
• Bob Israel: Responsible for renovating houses in Franklin Square

I also wish to than the following friends old and new, who gave of their talents and support to help this project become a reality:

Tarryn R., Susan F., John C., Heidi L., Cindy B., Fran D., Jodi F., Luke G, Chris C, Caroline D., Cynthia F., Andrea K., John O., Bill M., Naomi M-R., Cara M., Mary Ellen O 'L., Maureen W., Nicole E., Weezie F., Dave G., Bob and Theresa H., Sevey M.

And lastly, I wish to thank my family for their support and feedback on my most ambitious creative journey:

Klare and Matt I., Tina and Ray M., Lisa M., Anne C. Julianne C., Godmother Rae

Made in the USA
Middletown, DE
15 May 2025

75572276R00052